KIAM

Journey with young Henry, age 10, as nature reveals to him the wisdom of Kiam, a way of life that leads to health and fulfillment.

Catch the Current Publishing
Santa Monica, California
www.catchthecurrentpublishing.com

Also by Bill E. Goldberg

Prose

Protecting the Diamond:
Communicating Out of Your Comfort Zone (CD)

The "And" Principle:
Celebrating Self-Acceptance

Poetry

Catch the Current

Be Like the River

The Journey

KIAM ™

A Young Boy's Journey to Feeling Good

A Tale for Kids and Grown-Ups

By Bill E. Goldberg

Publisher's Website
www.catchthecurrentpublishing.com

Bill E. Goldberg has applied
to register KIAM™, an acronym, as a trademark.

Cover and illustrations by Bill E. Goldberg

Printed in the United States of America

First Printing, 2012

ISBN 978-0-9661461-4-1

Catch the Current Publishing

Dedication

That all baby oaks grow up
to be big, strong, glorious oak trees
with branches that streak
like lightning across the sky.

That all children, everywhere,
grow up to be
all that they can be.

Acknowledgment

To the spirit of life
that inspires me beyond measure.

Dear Reader,

I hope that you enjoy KIAM!

(Pronounced KEE-um.)

If there are words you don't understand, you can go to the glossary in the back of the book for a definition or explanation.

All my best,

Bill

KIAM

Once upon a time there was a little boy named Henry. He was ten years old and for much of his life he had been sick — a runny nose here, a cough there. He was not feeling good much of the time. How sad it was for Henry! Often he couldn't go to school and play outside with his friends. He'd see other children enjoying themselves and feel a yearning deep in his heart to be healthy and well. His family was very concerned about him. They had taken Henry to doctors and no one could figure out what was going on with him. Everyone was puzzled and frustrated about what to do.

One day when Henry had finally gotten over a long cold, his family decided to go camping. Henry, his older brother Ian, and his Mom and Dad all got in the car and drove into the mountains. When they arrived at the campground, they picked a wonderful campsite by a river. Everyone felt so good getting out of the city and being surrounded by the beauty of nature. They had arrived early in the day, so there was plenty of time to do something fun.

They decided to take a raft down the river and this is where their real adventure began. It was a warm day and soon they were all in the raft enjoying gliding, coasting, and relaxing in the sun. A gentle breeze combined with the sun to make the temperature just right. As they cascaded down the river, they were refreshed by the clean air and water. Just looking at the deep blue water made them feel clean inside. Henry leaned back against the side of the raft and gently put his hand in the water. It felt so good he got on his knees, put both hands in the water, and washed his face in it. What a rush! He felt exhilarated!

About a half an hour went by and everyone was talking and sipping the cold drinks they had brought. They felt like they were in heaven, and they were. Dad, who was steering the raft, noticed that a little way down the river a smaller stream broke off to the right. He was curious to see where it went so he veered to the right and they were off on a new adventure.

This tributary was smaller than the river yet was lovely in its own way. It moved slower and was very relaxing. Dad noticed that on his left there was a big boulder. He maneuvered the raft and started going around the big rock. He encountered a large eddy where the water was swirling round and round, caught between the boulder and the bank of the stream. The water was no longer flowing freely there.

Once again, Henry leaned back against the side of the raft and put his hand in the water. He quickly yanked it out this time because it felt all slimy and yucky. It felt dirty, with decaying leaves in it. He said to himself, "I'd never want to wash my face in that water. It would make me sick." All of a sudden a light bulb went off in his head. He thought to himself, "The river water that is moving is clean and I was excited to wash my face in it, yet this blocked water that isn't moving feels dirty and would make me sick." Then he thought, "I get sick a lot." "Click, click, click!" he heard inside his head. "Flowing... clean. Blocked... dirty." Henry felt that the river was speaking to him. He now was listening intently.

And then from the depths of the river he heard, "The key to being healthy is to '**K**eep **I**t **A**ll **M**oving.'" "Kiam, Kiam, Kiam" he heard the river repeat. Henry loved the sound of the word "Kiam." It was short and sweet sounding to his ears.

Then a big question came into his mind. How do I

keep things moving in my life? What does the river mean by Kiam? So Henry asked the river, "How do you do this? How do you keep things moving?" The river quickly answered saying, "If you listen really carefully and pay attention to nature, to the mountains, the birds, to all of nature's creatures and surroundings, they each will teach you a lesson about Kiam. Nature will teach you how to live in a way that works." The river said that if he *asked a question* to the mountain or birds, they might give him an answer if he could learn to speak their language. This idea made Henry feel very excited. He felt like he had a new friend in the river.

That night as darkness began to cover the land, Henry's Dad built a *small* teepee out of kindling wood. Henry knew that they would soon have a *great*, *big* campfire. He loved being with his family around a campfire at night. The sky would be black, he'd see thousands of stars, and the air would be cold and crisp. Sure enough, when the night came that's exactly how it was. His father lit the fire and in no time it was ablaze.

As Henry peered into the flames, his mind began to ponder. He felt a little sad thinking about how often he was sick. His mind went back to the river. He remembered that it had been talking to him that day. It wanted to help him stay well. It wanted to teach him the ways of vibrant health. It had told him to pay attention and listen to the things in nature, so he said to himself, "I wonder if this fire has a lesson for me?" Inwardly he asked the fire if it had any clues about Kiam, and then he got real quiet inside. He stared deeply into the fire and it began to cast a spell over him. The flames began to mesmerize him.

Once he was very relaxed, he heard the fire say, "I need oxygen to burn." Then he remembered his Dad earlier fanning the flames of the fire to make them bigger. The more oxygen they got, the bigger they became. He noticed that the flames were now *moving and dancing* like the wind. He began to think that he also needed to breathe more deeply, get lots of oxygen, and move and dance like the flames. Henry was sure that the fire had given him two important parts of Kiam. *Breathe and move. Breathe and move.* He now began to feel like the fire was his friend.

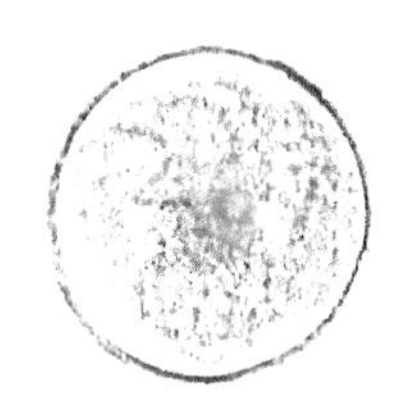

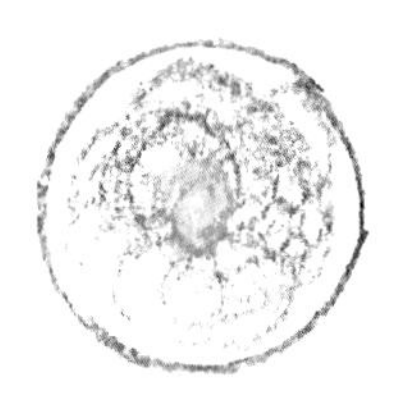

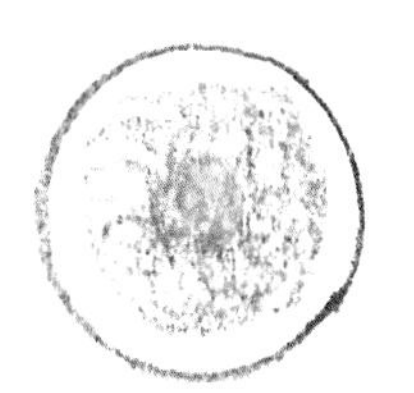

The next day Henry awoke excited to see what new answers would come to him today about Kiam. His Dad came to his tent and asked him if he'd like to take a walk. Henry, loving to spend time with his Dad, eagerly said, "Yes." As they ventured down the trail, they both noticed in the distance there were dark clouds forming. They looked ominous, foreboding. Suddenly, Henry saw lightning streaking across the sky. It was scary *and* it was beautiful. Now Henry was really excited. Then, as if the sky was angry, a thunderous, loud sound cracked the air. The earth shook a bit from the sound. Nature was putting on quite a show. Henry and his Dad thought it best to head back to camp before it started raining. They both quickly got into Henry's tent and then the rain came down like tears falling from the sky.

Then as fast as the lightning, thunder, and rain had come, they vanished and Henry cautiously peered out of his tent and looked towards the mountains. And guess what he saw? A gorgeous rainbow stretched its beautiful arms across two mountain peaks. What a sight! Everything looked clean after the rain and there was an unusual calm that surrounded the land. He noticed the sweet sound of the birds again trickling through the air.

So once again, Henry asked himself, "What is this weather teaching me?" The answer that came from deep in his heart was that as nature has many moods, so he should accept all of his moods. And that nature gracefully flows from one mood to another. The lightning brings the thunder and the thunder brings the rain. The thunder doesn't hold on to the thunder. It moves easily into the rain. He thought, "lightning…thunder…rain, lightning…thunder…rain." Henry remembered seeing children playing and how one minute they are happily playing and the next they are mad at each other, and then a few minutes later they are playing and laughing together again. *Kids tend to feel things and let them go.* He remembered times when he was angry or sad. He also remembered how relieved he felt *after* he got angry or sad. There was a calm after his emotional storms, just like there was after this storm. And just like the appearance of the rainbow, there is a reward for accepting his moods, his feelings.

Then he heard, "The promise and gift of feeling all of your feelings is the peace and beauty of the rainbow." He thought, "The voice of nature is so poetic!" He pondered, "If all those feelings stayed cramped up inside, they probably would make me sick." Certainly *accepting feelings* was part of the river of Kiam and being well! Henry was surely on his way to a wise heart. He was paying attention and the river was smiling at him.

The next morning Henry once again woke to the sweet sounds of the birds. They were singing their little hearts out! Henry closed his eyes and realized that each bird had a different song. He smiled and felt happy that nature was giving him more answers to his question about Kiam. The birds seemed healthy and joyful, and he realized they were teaching him that to be this way we need to express ourselves and *sing our own song*. Not the song of the bear or the lizard, nor the song of the mountain lion or the spider. Each creature is different and so are we.

He continued to watch the birds and saw them gathering little sticks for their nests. He saw the butterflies pollinating the flowers. An industrious little group of creatures was surrounding him! Clearly Kiam had to do with *expressing and creating*. Realizing this, Henry felt happy.

Now his Mom, needing to exercise and walk, asked little Henry to accompany her up the trail. Eager for another adventure, Henry got ready and began walking with his Mom. This time he got further up the trail. He had brought binoculars with him in case he saw any animals that he wanted to see close up.

As Henry was walking, he saw a mother bird swooping down over and into a nest that was high up in a tree. It was dramatic to see such a big bird swooping like this. Henry quickly took out his binoculars and focused in on the nest. And behold, he saw four little birds inside. He saw the mother bird feeding them, and the little ones were so hungry it was hard for them to take their turns. After they were all fed, Henry saw each little bird peer over the edge of the nest to the ground below. It was a long way down and the little birds quickly scampered back to the center of the nest. Then he saw them go to the edge once more, and again scamper to the center. Henry asked his Mom what they were doing and she said that they were getting ready to fly for the first time and were scared.

A question entered Henry's curious mind. "What are they teaching me?" The answer came to him that *to fly you must jump*, you must take chances, you must take risks. He thought, "Definitely taking chances, *taking risks* is also a part of the great adventure of Kiam."

Henry and his Mom started walking back on the trail to the campsite enjoying each other's company. As they were walking, Henry saw something moving in the tall grass next to the trail. He got startled, scared, and jumped back suddenly. He thought it was a rattlesnake and he knew they were poisonous. Henry then pointed out the snake to his Mom. She knew a lot about snakes because she had studied biology. She told Henry that this was a garden snake and not poisonous. It looks like a rattlesnake, she said, yet it's very different. *Hearing this, everything changed for Henry. His fear turned into excitement!*

And as they continued walking, Henry heard the river say, "In your life, don't turn garden snakes into rattlers." He started thinking about fear and how he had let it stop him from doing many things and he felt sad. Then he heard the river speak again. It said, "Fear is there to protect you from *real danger* and it is not there to stop you from doing what you want and need to do!"

Henry felt deep in his stomach that dealing with fear was a big part of keeping everything moving, so he asked the river if it could tell him one more thing. And the river spoke, saying "Fear sometimes grows when you are alone in the dark. So take someone's hand and turn on the lights!" Henry liked this. Henry thought, "*Managing fear* was certainly a part of Kiam," and he felt a surge of power well up inside himself.

The next evening the family once again huddled around the campfire. They each put a folding chair right next to the fire to stay warm, making a little circle around it. Everyone was quiet. No one was saying a word. Then Henry's Dad asked Ian about the short raft trip he had taken by himself that afternoon. Dad's question and Ian's story broke the silence, and Henry noticed because the river had earlier talked to him about *the power of questions*.

Ian shared how he went way down the river until it got real calm. He stood up in the raft and took out his binoculars. Soon he saw a sight he would never forget. He saw a big brown bear scratching on the trunk of a tree. The bear looked at him with great interest. Then Ian noticed three little baby bears come out from behind the trees. They were so cute that he got very excited and almost fell out of the raft! Henry loved hearing Ian's story.

After Ian finished his story, Henry started to ponder. He was used to thinking about Kiam and the river, so he naturally started wondering about his

Dad's questioning Ian about his trip. He realized that that *one question changed everything*. Just one question created *a small opening* through which Ian's entire story got to be told. Henry found this idea exciting!

Then again he heard the river speak to him, saying "*Questions, curiosity, and communication* keep everything moving." All three words made a "Kh" sound. "Kh, Kh, Kh," he heard in his head. Henry liked to make up games and was beginning to have fun with words. He started thinking about communication. He thought about how a week earlier his Mom had come home and was being very quiet around the house. Henry had started to get uncomfortable, wondering if she was quiet because she was upset with him for doing something wrong. So he had asked her why she was quiet and she explained that it was because she wasn't feeling well and that it had nothing to do with him. Hearing this, Henry relaxed. "The power of talking," he thought.

The following day Ian came to Henry's tent and asked him to come and climb trees with him. Henry was surprised because Ian usually wasn't very friendly towards him. Excited, Henry and Ian began looking for good trees. They found a huge sycamore that had low branches and they started to climb. When they got mid-way up the tree, they had a great view of the river.

With loving concern, Ian asked Henry how he was feeling, and again Henry noticed how he was treating him differently. Over the years, Ian had occasionally been angry and resentful of Henry for being sick. It limited the family going camping and doing other fun things. Henry asked Ian why he was being so nice to him. "What has changed?" he asked him. Ian explained that he had been talking about his feelings with their Mom and Dad, and had understood that Henry was doing the best he could and that he wasn't intentionally trying to disrupt the family. They talked about understanding and forgiveness, and somehow all of this unloaded a burden from Ian. He felt closer to Henry and more accepting of him.

After experiencing this change in his brother, Henry once again started to ponder and think about Kiam. He wondered if *understanding and forgiveness* were part of keeping everything moving. He thought maybe judging others could keep him stuck in the past and he knew that being stuck in the past was the opposite of keeping everything moving. Henry sat in the tree with his back supported by a large branch and he thought how much he had learned about Kiam in just a few days.

But now he felt tired of all this searching and needed a break from his quest. So he got an inner tube and took a short ride down the river by himself, taking a snack and a bottle of water with him. After journeying down the river for a little while, he went on land and found a delightful spot to put down his towel and nap in the shade of a big oak tree.

He had a beautiful dream while he napped. In his dream he was healthy, feeling good, and had lots of friends. He was eating well and playing often. In his dream he was happy, and he awoke full of energy. That night after a wonderful dinner, his family prepared a tasty dessert with fresh berries topped with crunchy walnuts. Then they all shared stories gathered around the campfire. Once again Henry felt like he was in heaven, and he was.

The next morning Henry wasn't sure what he wanted to do. So he walked down a trail that followed the river. He then found a great spot to rest. He sat quietly listening to the wind in the trees. He listened to the wind with his eyes closed and soon noticed that he felt like he was deep in a well inside himself.

From this *deep well* he heard the trees speaking to him. He heard them say, "We can teach you about stillness, just like the river has been teaching you about movement." The words "stillness" *and* "movement" kept repeating in his mind. What was the relationship between the two, he wondered? And hearing the question, the trees answered, "If you learn to be still, you'll know how to move and how to act." Henry pondered, "There certainly is a lot to think about here."

Then instantly from the stillness he knew what he wanted to do with his day. He wanted to search through the forest with his Dad, find some bamboo, and carve out a flute. Henry wanted to be able to make sounds like the birds. Excitement flooded his little body and he felt joy. *He realized that stillness can lead to action that feels good!* Then the trees said they had one more very important thing to tell him, and Henry was eagerly listening. And the trees spoke, saying "Going to the well will help make you well." Henry, so wanting to be healthy, thought for a moment about what the trees had just said and felt hope in his heart.

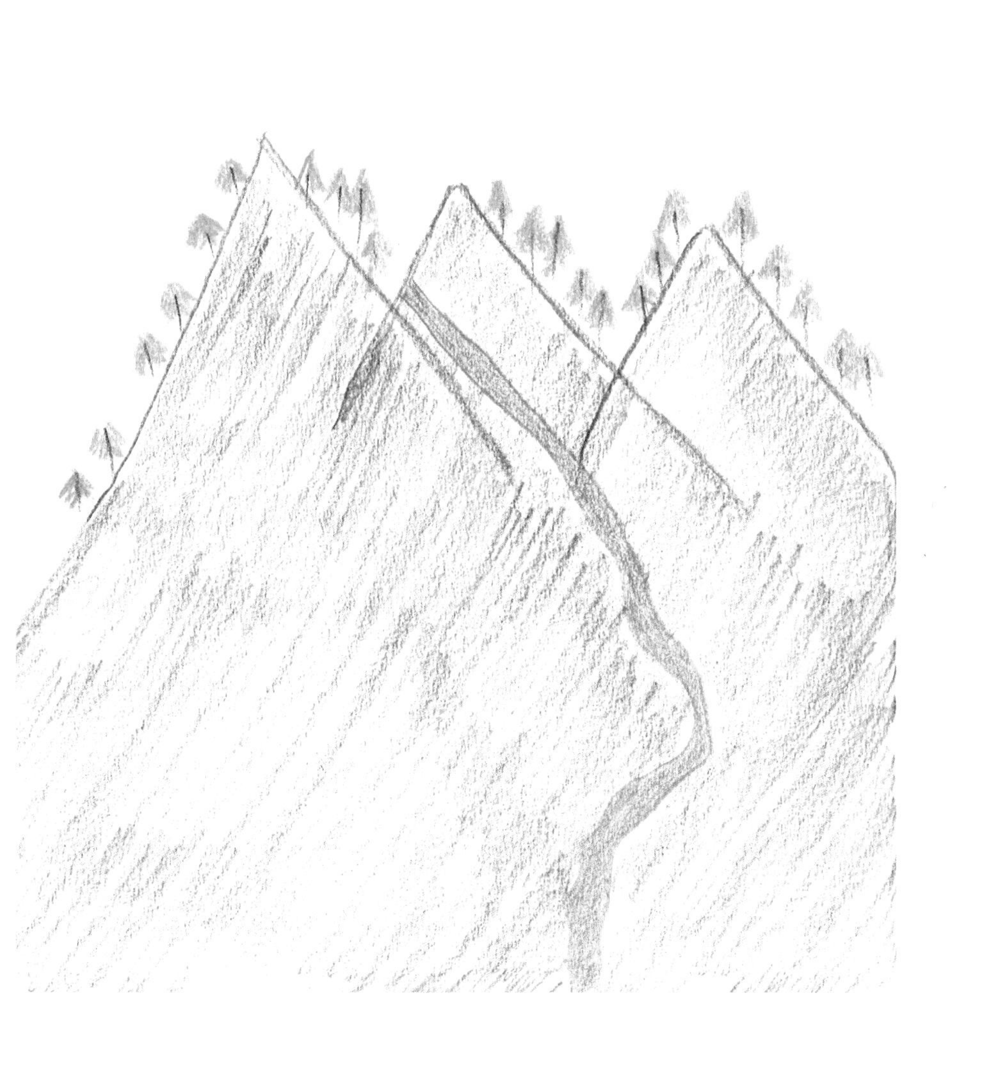

Back to the campsite he went, and found his Dad lounging in a hammock between two trees. Henry loved seeing him relaxing, for he worked so hard and gave so much to the family. He asked his Dad if it was hard on him to go to work everyday. He said at times it was difficult, *and* it also made him very happy to give. He liked feeling needed. Then a light bulb went off again in Henry's little head. *Giving* was without a doubt part of Kiam, he thought. It kept everything moving. Thinking of giving, he remembered how happy he was several weeks ago sharing some of his poems with his class at school. He saw how much the class loved hearing them. The whole experience seemed to create a circle. *Kiam was like a circle*, he thought.

After spending the day with his Dad carving a wonderful flute, Henry was hungry. So he had a relaxing dinner and talked for hours with his family around the campfire. Then, being very tired, he was ready to go to sleep. It was the last night of Henry's vacation. He got into his tent and soon was comfortable in bed. He loved being in bed in the woods listening to the quiet. He looked up at the stars through his window and felt the mystery of it all. Henry soon fell into a deep sleep and woke up very refreshed. He felt as if the mountains had given him something during the night. He thought that if people lived in nature, surrounded by beauty, they'd probably be happier and get along better!

That morning after Henry got dressed, he remembered that he had had a dream that night. He dreamt that the spirit of the mountain had come to him and asked if he had any more questions. Henry did have a question and asked the spirit of the mountain, "Is it easy to practice Kiam?" The spirit of the mountain said that the stronger and more self-confident a person is, the easier it is to do the practice, to feel and communicate and create and risk. The spirit of the mountain said that it was *very important* to be gentle with yourself when starting to practice Kiam and not judge how much you can do. As you build your sense of strength and are more confident, you will be able to do more. The spirit of the mountain then said, “All things begin small. Each tree starts out as a little seed.” Henry felt encouraged and knew he would start right where he was.

It was now the last day of their vacation, and the whole family took a long raft trip all the way to the sea and enjoyed spending the day at the ocean. The day was glorious with the beaming sun and the warmth of the sand on their feet. Any last little bit of tension from their city lives melted into the ocean sands. *Now Henry was really feeling healthy for the first time in years!* Tears filled his eyes. Tears of gratitude. He welcomed his tears knowing that feeling them was part of the great kingdom of Kiam.

He then took a walk down the beach by himself and found a spot on a small hill that overlooked the ocean. He could also see the river from this hill, emptying into the sea. Henry relaxed there for awhile and started to think about the adventures of his camping trip. He thought about what he had learned from the river and the fire, from the birds and the butterflies, from his father, mother and brother, from the storm and the snake, the trees and the mountain. He felt that his prayers and questions about how to keep things moving and be healthy had been answered. And as he sat on the hill by the sea overlooking the river, he once again entered the well of silence and his mind became quiet. *And he had a vision.* He saw many small rivers, tributaries, merging with one big river, and each one represented a part of Kiam. Then he saw the big river merging with the sea. Henry felt connected to everything and once again was happy in his heart.

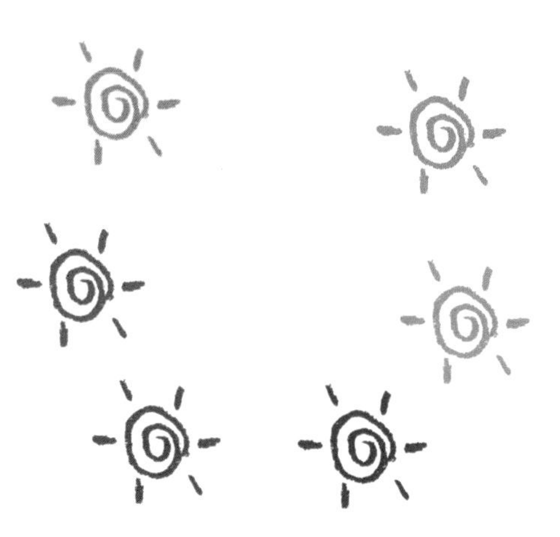

Henry's Journey to Health and Fulfillment

Lessons he learned from ...

The River

"The key to being healthy is to '**K**eep **I**t **A**ll **M**oving.'" "Kiam, Kiam, Kiam," he heard the river repeat.

The Fire

He noticed that the flames were now moving and dancing like the wind.

Henry was sure that the fire had given him two important parts of Kiam. *Breathe and move. Breathe and move.*

The Storm

"... as nature has many moods, so he should accept all of his moods."

"The promise and gift of feeling all of your feelings is the peace and beauty of the rainbow."

The Birds and the Butterflies

"... we need to express ourselves and *sing our own song* ... Clearly Kiam had to do with *expressing and creating."*

The Baby Birds

The answer came to him that *to fly you must jump*, you must take chances, you must take risks.

The Snake and the River

“Fear is there to protect you from *real danger* and it is not there to stop you from doing what you want and need to do!”

“In your life, don’t turn garden snakes into rattlers.”

“Fear sometimes grows when you are alone in the dark. So take someone’s hand and turn on the lights!”

His Dad and the River
(His Dad’s one question to Ian)

“Questions, curiosity, and communication keep everything moving.”

Just one question created *a small opening* through which Ian’s entire story got to be told.

Ian
(Being nice to Henry)

He wondered if *understanding and forgiveness* were part of keeping everything moving.

The Trees

"If you learn to be still, you'll know how to move and how to act."

"Going to this well will help make you well."

His Dad
(Giving to the Family)

Giving was without a doubt part of Kiam, he thought. It kept everything moving.

Kiam was like a circle, he thought.

The Spirit of the Mountain

"... it is *very important* to be gentle with yourself when starting to practice Kiam and not judge how much you can do ... All things begin small. Each tree starts out as a little seed."

Glossary

accompany (v) – to go with as a companion

cascade (v) – to flow fast and in larger amounts

curiosity (n) – an eagerness to know about something or someone

eddy (n) – a movement in a flowing stream of liquid or gas in which the current doubles back to form a small whirl.

endorse (v) – to give formal approval or permission for something

essence (n) – the most important element or feature of something

exhilarate (v) – to feel happy and alive

foreboding (adj) – a feeling that something bad is going to happen

glorious (adj) – exceptionally lovely, beautiful in a way that inspires wonder and joy

hammock (n) – a hanging bed made of canvas or netting and suspended between two supports

Kiam (n) – a way of life that leads to health and fulfillment.

v – verb   n – noun   adj – adjective

lounge (v) – lie or sit lazily

maneuver (v) – to move in a skilled way

mesmerize (v) – to fascinate someone or absorb all of their attention

ominous (adj) – warning or suggesting that something undesirable is likely to happen

pollinate (v) – to transfer pollen and fertilize a plant

ponder (v) – to think about something carefully over a period of time

quest (n) – an adventurous journey, a search for something, especially a long or difficult one

spontaneous (adj) – done or said freely and naturally without planning

sycamore (n) – a type of maple tree

tributary (n) – a stream, river, or glacier that joins a larger stream, river, glacier, or lake

vanish (v) – to disappear suddenly

venture (v) – to dare to do something

v – verb   n – noun   adj – adjective

Bill E. Goldberg is a licensed Marriage and Family Therapist who shares here, for children and adults, the essence of the life philosophy he developed over twenty years as a counselor and teacher. He has written extensively and his communications CD, *Protecting the Diamond* has been endorsed by *New York Times* best-selling authors, **John Bradshaw** (*Homecoming*) and **Dr. Thomas Gordon** (*Parent Effectiveness Training, P.E.T.*).

Bill is a great admirer of the creative process. Writing, dancing, and dwelling in nature are some of the ways he appreciates this process.

He has dedicated much of his career to children, helping them grow up more easily realizing their potential.

You can contact him at:
bill@catchthecurrentpublishing.com.

To order the following books or CD,
or to see a beautiful website, visit
www.catchthecurrentpublishing.com:

Kiam: A Young Boy's Journey to Feeling Good

Journey with young Henry, age 10, as he learns from nature how to be healthy and find fulfillment. ($16.95)

The "And" Principle: Celebrating Self-Acceptance

The "And" Principle contains reflections, poems, and questions on the theme of accepting all parts of yourself. It is a big hug in the form of a book! ($15.95)

Protecting the Diamond: Communicating Out of Your Comfort Zone (CD)

Bill shares here a powerful communication system that he developed over twenty years as a counselor, teacher, and writer. This system has helped thousands of people create thriving, fulfilling relationships. It includes practical and effective tools for protecting the love in your life. ($15.95)

To read a chapter from *The "And" Principle*, or **to listen to sound-tracks** from *Protecting the Diamond*, visit www.catchthecurrentpublishing.com.

CPSIA information can be obtained
at www.ICGtesting.com
Printed in the USA
LVIW021909071112
306266LV00002B

* 9 7 8 0 9 6 6 1 4 6 1 4 1 *